White Water!

Penn Mullin

A PERSPECTIVES BOOK
Academic Therapy Publications
Novato, California

Gratitude is expressed to Helen Young, River Guide with the Nonesuch Whitewater Rafting Company of Sonoma County, California, for her valuable assistance is providing authentic rafting information for this book.

Art Supervisor: Herb Heidinger
Cover Design and Interior Illustrations: Joe Wallace

International Standard Book Number: 0-87879-319-4

8 7 6 5 4 3 2 1 0 9
5 4 3 2 1 0 9 8 7 6

Contents

CHAPTER 1

Terror at the Bend

"Here we go! Follow me!" Robb pushed his raft away from the dock and rowed out into the river current.

Kara watched her brother from her raft. He rowed well, with long, smooth strokes. This was his third summer as a river guide. He was more at home in a raft than anywhere else.

Kara pushed off from the dock to follow Robb. Smooth and deep, she told herself as she dipped the long oars into the water. She wanted to do everything just right today. Robb had finally agreed to let her take a raft down the river herself. This was her chance to show him she was good enough to be a raft guide this summer.

The sun was not yet on the river. Kara shivered in the T-shirt she wore under her life jacket. She began to hear the roar of the rapids ahead in the canyon. Her heart began to pound. Was it too soon? Was she really ready to try it alone? Devil's Chute was just ahead. Here the river became a thin stream of angry white water as it raced between the steep canyon walls.

Kara braced herself on the wooden rowing seat at the center of the raft. "Point your nose to the trouble," she told herself. This was one of the oldest rules in rafting. She put her boat in the center of the current and faced the white water ahead. The Chute was a real test of skill. Kara would have to work hard to keep the huge waves from smashing the raft up onto the canyon walls. And there were always the deadly "brownies" to watch for. "Brownies" were huge boulders lying just under the water. They could flip a raft in an instant.

She was coming into the Chute now. Huge waves pounded against the canyon walls and sent cold white spray crashing down on the raft. "Slow down, slow down," Kara told herself. "Move a little sideways in the current. Swing the bow left, then backrow." She leaned forward on the oars and stretched out her arms. Then she dipped deep with the oars and pulled back with one long smooth move. It worked. The raft slowed its speed.

Then she saw it—the huge gray-green boulder

dead ahead. She had to turn—fast. Pivot, pivot! She pulled hard on her right oar while she pushed on the left. The raft turned and sailed past the rock. She'd made it! But there was no time to think about it. Another boulder ahead on the left! Another double oar turn, another miss. The cold spray kept blinding Kara as she fought to keep the raft in the center of the Chute.

Suddenly her raft raced into a wide straight stretch of water. She was out of the Chute! There were no boulders to be seen. Only rows and rows of "haystacks" —large round pools of water at the foot of a rapid. They usually meant deep water. Kara relaxed and let her raft run straight down the middle of the river. Just like a roller coaster, she told herself.

Robb was about thirty feet ahead of her downriver. He turned and waved. Had he seen her come down the Chute, Kara wondered. She hoped he had. She knew he wasn't sure a girl would make a good river guide. She had to change his mind.

Kara leaned back for a moment and raised her face to the warm spring sun. She felt the soft wind's pull at her hair. If only this day could last forever! This was what she loved. For this moment she felt as if the river was completely hers. She hoped the summer would never end.

Then she heard Robb yelling at her. "Kara! We're at the bend! Get to the inside shore! Fast!"

The bend—already? She'd thought she had plenty of time to get ready for it. But she was too late and she knew it. The current had her. It was pulling her raft to the outside shore. Kara's throat felt tight. She could barely breathe. *Inside* shore always on a turn. One of the oldest rules on the river. And she had forgotten. She pulled on the oars with all her strength. But she knew it was no use. The river was stronger—always. The raft moved out towards the outside bank. She heard Robb shouting something but could not hear the words. She fought to swing her bow around to face downriver. Then she saw it—the huge gray rock straight ahead of her raft. Pivot, pivot — swing the bow around! But her timing was off. Her pivot was too early. The current swept her right into the rock! The raft rode straight up the rock and flipped over backwards. Kara was trapped underneath!

CHAPTER 2

Trapped!

Everything was dark. Kara's mouth filled with icy cold water. She fought for air. Her heart pounded with fear. Her hands tore at the bottom of the raft. Where was the edge? Which way was which? Her lungs felt as though they would burst. Suddenly her hands found the edge of the raft. She clawed her way up towards the sunlight. She took in deep breaths of fresh air. She was free of the raft. Her lifejacket carried her along in the swift current. Her body was shaking. She had no control over it. She was numb. Someone was shouting. Finally she heard the words, "Get your feet in front of you! Out in front! Kara, can you hear me? There are rocks ahead. Go down feet first!"

She wanted to do what Robb was saying. But her body would not obey. She was swept along backwards in the current. Robb was downstream about thirty feet. He had pulled behind a rock, a calm place out of the river current. He was getting ready to throw a rope to Kara. But could she catch it? Could she hold onto it? Robb was sure she was going into shock from the cold water. He had to get this rope to her before she passed out. He could see Kara floating towards him. Her body bobbed along backwards, bumping into rocks along the way.

"Kara!" Robb shouted. "Catch this line! I'm going to throw it to you." Had she heard him? There was no way to tell. She was almost even with him. He had to throw the line now or miss his chance. He braced himself against the rowing seat and threw the line. It sailed out over Kara's head, then floated down towards her. A perfect throw. But would she grab it? Robb held his breath. Suddenly he saw Kara's arm reach slowly towards the rope.

"Grab it, Kara! Grab it!" he shouted.

The rope went tight. She had it! Robb knew he had to work fast. He began to pull Kara towards him. She was like a limp rag doll in the water. But she held on. And at last Robb had her at the side of his raft.

Her skin was a bluish color, and her eyes were dazed. He pulled her cold shivering body aboard the raft. This was hypothermia—he was sure of it. Every river guide is trained to be ready for this silent killer that has claimed more lives than any rapids ever did. Hypothermia kills by dropping a person's body temperature to as low as 77°. At this point, the heart stops working. People with hypothermia have to be made warm as fast as

"Catch this line!"

possible if they are to live. Robb wrapped his spare jacket around Kara as she lay on the bottom of the raft. Then he rowed quickly towards shore.

Robb pulled into a sandy stretch of land and lifted Kara's limp body out of the raft. He laid her down on a patch of sand. The first thing to do was to strip off her wet clothes. Robb then grabbed a small wool blanket from his first-aid chest. He wrapped it around his sister and himself. Kara's body would not stop shaking. He felt her pulse. It was very weak. He held her body tight against his own. This was the fastest way to warm up a hypothermic person. Slowly he felt Kara's body begin to relax. Her shivering finally stopped. Her pulse rate was better. The bluish color of her skin was going away. But Robb still held her close against him. He lost all track of time. Then he heard voices shouting, coming closer.

"Robb! Kara! Are you OK?" It was Pete and Jim on their raft. They pulled into shore and raced over to where Robb and Kara lay.

CHAPTER 3

Time Ashore

"Each of you must wear a life jacket at all times. It could save your life." Kara stood on the dock talking to a group that was starting out on a raft trip down the river. "And be sure to keep on your tennis shoes. River rocks can be sharp. Have I got everybody signed in now?"

"Yep. All here," said one of the guys.

"OK. Ed's going to be your guide today. I'll turn you over to him now. Have a great trip, everybody!" Kara waved and walked away from the dock. Ed started talking to the group on raft safety. Kara knew this talk by heart. She'd learned all the rules last winter so she'd be ready to guide this summer. But that was all before the accident. She still shivered when she thought about it. The raft coming down on top of her. Fighting for air. Not being able to get out from under the raft. That had happened four weeks ago. But it all seemed like yesterday to Kara.

She'd had to stay in bed for awhile after the accident. It seemed as though the hypothermia had taken away all her strength. And it was a long time until she came down to the river again. She hadn't wanted to be anywhere near it. Then she started going down to the dock in the mornings with Robb. She'd just sit there and watch the raft trips start out. Then some of the guides asked her to help them get their groups ready to go. This had become her regular job in the mornings. It was OK; it was something to do. But everybody could tell Kara was not the same person she had been before the accident. She had lost her sparkle. She never laughed any more.

After Ed's raft took off, Kara sat down on the dock. She felt someone come up behind her.

"Mind if I sit down?" It was Cy, the owner of the rafting company. He smiled down at Kara. His kind face was deeply tanned and lined from long years on the river. "How's it going, kid? It's good to see you down here again. We missed you."

Cy's words sounded wonderful to Kara. She knew he didn't talk much.

"Thanks. I'm doing OK, I guess," Kara said. She stared hard at the old boards in the dock.

She knew what Cy was going to say next. He was going to tell her she'd better forget any ideas about being a guide.

"You've had a pretty rough time," Cy began. He slowly tapped some tobacco into his pipe. "Getting pinned under a raft is mean business. I should know."

Kara turned to Cy in surprise.

"It was a long time ago. After a big rain. The river was high, too high. The wind was bad. I took a raft downriver to check out the storm damage. You know that bend they call Dead Man? I came whipping around that and smashed right into a big redwood that had blown into the river. Flipped me right over." Cy closed his eyes. "I'll never forget how it was being under that raft. Not knowing which way to swim. Running out of air. Well, *you* sure as heck know what it's like. No picnic, that's for sure."

Kara couldn't believe Cy was telling her this. She didn't think he'd ever wrecked a raft. Not Cy. He'd been rafting longer than anyone on the river.

"How'd you get out?" Kara wanted Cy to keep on talking.

"Just like you did, I guess. Felt my way to the edge of the raft and then came on up. But, boy, was that water cold! And, boy, was I scared! Took me a long while to get over the whole thing. Didn't go near the river for a long time. No sir."

"Really? You didn't?" Kara stared at Cy. Suddenly she didn't feel so dumb any more. And she knew being scared was OK.

"Well, I better get to work." Cy stood up and stretched. "Got some paddle tips need fixing. Want to give me a hand?"

Kara couldn't believe it. Cy always worked alone at his tool bench. She sprang to her feet. "Sure. I'd love to help."

Several oak paddles were lined up on the dock. Cy picked one up by the handle and pointed to the paddle end. "See how it's split here? Here's how we fix it." He sat down at his tool bench. Then he took a sharp knife and cut out a little rectangle around the split wood. He had a pile of new pieces of wood stacked on the shelf. He took one of these and fit it into the hole in the paddle with strong glue.

"There. We'll let that set awhile. Then it'll be good as new. Here, you try one." Cy held out a paddle towards Kara.

Kara sat down on the dock and placed the paddle across her knees. Cy handed her a knife. Then Kara began carefully cutting into the paddle blade.

"See the newspaper this morning?" Cy asked as he started on another paddle. "More stuff about that dam they want to build."

Kara noticed the angry tone in Cy's voice. All the river guides were angry—and scared. The government wanted to dam up the Stevenson River and turn it into a huge lake. That way it would be easier for farmers to use the water for their crops. Damming up the Stevenson would mean the end of white water. The end of rafting.

"I saw it. I can't believe they'd really do it, Cy. It would just be crazy to ruin the river." Kara carefully fitted the new piece of wood into the paddle.

"The government's pretty strong." Cy reached over to help Kara smooth in the new wood. "This could be the last summer for white water."

The last summer! It couldn't be! "If only we could get those high-up people to come and see what they'd be destroying by damming the river," Kara said. "We've got to get people to pay attention to this river before it's too late."

"Right you are. But what can we do?" Cy tapped the ashes out of his pipe. "Here, let me see how you're doing there." He took the paddle from Kara.

"Looks pretty darned good! Why don't you try a couple more?" Cy handed Kara two more paddles.

She couldn't believe it! He liked what she'd done. She hadn't messed up. Suddenly she felt wonderful. Better than she had in a long long time.

They sat on the dock until late morning, mending paddles. They didn't talk much, but Kara didn't mind. It just felt good to be sitting there working next to Cy.

Finally Cy stood up and stretched. "That's enough for today. Just leave the rest of them, Kara. Say, I've got a new raft I want to try out. Want to come along?"

Kara felt her stomach get tense. Her face felt hot all over. Once she would have given anything to go rafting with Cy. Now all she could feel was this awful lump in her throat. Was she ready yet to get back on the river? Was it too soon?

CHAPTER 4

The Inside Bank

"You go get the life jackets. I'll meet you at the raft," Cy told Kara. Then he walked off down the dock.

Kara did as Cy had said. You always did as Cy said down here at the dock. Then she joined him beside the big gray raft at the water's edge.

Cy was running his hands over the sides of the new raft. "Isn't she a beauty? There's nothing this raft can't do." Cy started putting the ten-foot oak oars into the oarlocks on either side of the raft. Then he picked up a spare oar and placed it in the raft, too.

Kara stood there staring down at the raft. There was still time to back out. She could say she was sick or something.

"Hand me those life jackets, will you? And go ahead and get in. We might as well get started. I can't wait to see how this raft likes the water." Cy started putting on his life jacket. Kara did the same. Then she sat down in the bow of the raft. Cy settled onto the rowing seat, facing downriver.

"OK. We're off!" Cy pushed away from the dock.

Kara felt the raft move out into the river current. Cy applied power to the oars smoothly and steadily with solid, deep strokes.

"Can you feel how light she is? And see how easily she turns?" Cy moved the raft along in the current, trying out all kinds of quick movements with his oars. Kara sat watching him and trying to block out all other thoughts from her mind.

Then she heard the loud roar of the white water. That awful tight feeling seemed to be filling her whole chest.

They were going into the Chute. Kara grabbed the safety line in the bow. Her heart pounded as the big waves crashed against the canyon walls and sent spray flying into her face.

Cy kept the raft in the center of the Chute, pointing his bow downstream. He scooted the raft neatly around each boulder.

"Whoopee! See how fast she turns!" Cy shouted. "Ready for the roller coaster?"

The raft raced down into the wide flat stretch

of deep water at the end of the Chute. Cy let the raft run free, rolling up and over the smooth waves. His eyes shone with excitement. His face and beard sparkled with the cold river spray.

"Come on. Sit here. You've got to try out this raft. Wait till you see how she rows." Cy pulled Kara gently into the rowing seat. Her heart was pounding. Her mouth felt dry.

"Try her out in this nice calm stretch here. Just keep her in the center where the water's deep." Cy got up and moved into the bow seat. Kara knew he wasn't coming back. Her hands closed around the oars. The hard wooden handles felt strange. It had been a long time.

She began to work the oars gently, keeping the raft in the center of the river. Now she knew what Cy meant—the raft was so light! She felt as though she could row with her fingertips!

All at once she remembered—the bend! She had almost forgotten it—again! She had to work the raft over to the inside shore. The current was much stronger now. She could feel it pulling her towards the outside part of the bend.

"Push deep with that left oar!" Cy shouted. "Back with the right. That's the way. Keep it up. Move towards the inside."

What if I can't get over? What if I swing wide

and hit that rock again? Kara fought the current. Her shoulders ached. Why had she ever come on the river again? She was going to mess up, just like before. Suddenly Kara felt the raft pull itself away from the current and swing to the inside shore. Her body began to shake as she let up on the oars. They had made it around the bend.

All at once she remembered—the bend!

"There you go! You did just fine." Cy smiled at Kara. Then he looked towards the shore. "Hey, we're pretty near to where I left the truck. Let's head into shore."

"The truck's here? So close to base?" Now Kara understood. Cy had planned the whole thing! He'd wanted her to try going around the bend again. Testing out the new raft was just an excuse to get her out on the river. Suddenly Kara was excited. She'd made it around the bend! And it felt great to be on the river again. She grinned at Cy and headed the raft towards shore.

"Hey, let's have a look at those hands. You were really working those oars."

"Oh, that's OK," Kara said.

"Yeah. I guess you better get used to it. All good river guides get blisters once in awhile."

River guide! He'd said river guide! Kara couldn't believe it. "Cy, do you mean it? You'll let me guide? This summer?"

"Sure. Of course, there are a few more things I want to make sure you know. Got to do a lot of runs so you can almost do it with your eyes closed. But, hey, are you gonna let us float right by my truck over there?" Cy laughed. "It's a long walk back upriver!"

CHAPTER 5

The Graveyard

"Ready for the Graveyard today?" Cy asked Kara as they carried the oars over to the raft.

Oh, no, Kara thought to herself. He's been saving that run for last. The worst part on the river. Full of boulders and holes. This would be a true test of how well she could handle a raft alone. She could feel herself starting to get tense. Was she ready for this? Cy had been testing her on all kinds of water for the past two weeks. He'd taught her lots of tricks. But, best of all, he'd taught her how to read the water. To know where an underwater rock might lie, to know where the worst holes were likely to be.

"OK, Cy, I guess I'm ready. What are we waiting for?" Kara put on her life jacket. She sounded much braver than she felt.

Cy sat down in the front of the raft. Kara took her place at the oars. She began rowing downstream towards the Chute. She was used to the roar of the white water now. But each time she heard it, her heart began to pound. She'd run the Chute many times in the past few weeks. Now she felt at home in the narrow strip of angry white water. It seemed much easier now to keep her bow facing into the waves. And she knew

"Ready for the Graveyard today?"

where the "brownies" were. Her raft moved through the Chute and downriver towards the Graveyard.

"Better and better every time." Cy smiled at Kara from the bow. "You're ready for the Graveyard, kid. Let's go!"

Kara rowed steadily downstream. She listened hard for the first sound of the Graveyard rapids.

Cy put his feet up on the first-aid box. "Did you see that government fellow hanging around yesterday? He says he was up here to check on the road. Some dumb thing about making the road wider. That's so they can bring in big trucks for making that dam. Bet you anything that's why they want to widen the road. Now ain't that the limit? Ruin the river *and* run some four-lane highway through the forest." Cy spat into the water.

"You think they're gonna build that dam for sure, Cy? Don't they know how many people are against it?" Kara felt the river current growing stronger. And now she began to hear the roar of white water downriver. She tightened her grip on the oars.

"Sure they know people don't want the dam. People have written at least a thousand letters to the governor about saving the river. Doesn't seem to be doing much good." Cy looked downriver towards the white water.

What if this *was* the last summer for the river, Kara thought. What if this was the only summer she would ever guide on the Stevenson? Suddenly she saw the first big boulders of the Graveyard ahead. Now the only thing in her mind was to take her raft safely through them.

The current grew faster and faster. The raft raced towards the boulders. They seemed to be all around her. And it was up to Kara to find a safe course through them. Cy must not guess how scared she was.

She had to slow her speed. The raft had to be turned sideways just a little in the current. Kara pulled back on her right oar and felt the raft turn gently to the side. She had turned just enough. The raft had slowed down. Cy gave her a thumbs-up signal and grinned. So far so good, she thought to herself. Her eyes searched the foaming water ahead for any hidden rocks. Suddenly she saw a huge brownish-green shape dead ahead!

CHAPTER 6

White Water Ahead!

Pivot! Pivot! Get the bow straight. Kara knew what she had to do. But was there time? The raft raced straight towards the boulder. Kara pushed and pulled hard on the oars. Come on, raft, turn, will you? Why aren't you turning?

"You can do it!" Cy shouted. "Lean into those oars! That's the way!" The raft suddenly turned away from the rock. It raced by with only inches to spare.

"Great going!" Cy yelled above the roar of the water. "That was a mean one! Better get back to the center." He pointed to another huge boulder ahead on the right of the raft. Kara was ready for this one. With a quick double-oar turn she moved the raft neatly around the rock.

"Ya-hoo!" Cy yelled. "Way to go!"

Kara felt wonderful. She was ready for anything now. She moved the raft swiftly from side to side among the rocks.

Then she heard Cy shout, "Rock dead ahead! We're going to hit bow-on. Hold tight!" He jumped towards the center of the raft.

Kara felt a sickening bump as the raft slammed into the rock. How had it happened? She'd been watching so carefully. She felt the raft stop for a second. Now was her chance to spin it off the rock with her turn strokes. She pulled hard on the oars. The raft slipped off the rock and raced back into the current. They'd been lucky. Many rafts would have filled with water and been sucked under if they had hit a rock that way. Kara's hands were shaking as she gripped the oars.

"Lot of holes coming up!" Cy yelled from the front of the raft. "Keep that bow downstream."

Kara held tight to the oars. Holes were no fun to get stuck in. They could flip a raft in an instant. And they were very hard to see. There could be bad ones just behind a boulder or beside a fallen tree.

Kara turned her raft sharply to avoid a huge green boulder. The raft shot into the white swirl of foam behind the rock and stuck there. A hole! Kara's eyes were wide with fear. Suddenly the raft jumped back out into the main current.

Kara's eyes searched wildly for the next boulder in her path.

"We're through it! That's the last of the boulders along here. Good going! Now we can relax. Head for the bridge. That's where I've got the truck." Cy put his feet up on the ice chest and lit his pipe.

It felt good to row in the slow deep water and know that the bridge was close by. Kara looked at Cy sitting in the bow. What was he thinking? How many more times would he be taking her out to practice? The summer would be over before she'd ever have a chance to guide. And what if this was the last summer for the river?

"Don't suppose you'd want to take a group out on this raft tomorrow," Cy said.

"Really? You mean it? Of course, I would! Oh, Cy, thanks! I can't believe it." Finally Cy thought she was ready. She would have her own group to guide down the river. She would be in charge. It was a big job. But Kara knew she was ready for it. Cy thought she was, too. And that made everything right. She rowed hard and fast towards the bridge. She could hardly wait to share her good news with Robb.

CHAPTER 7

River Guide

Kara and Cy drove the truck into the base parking lot. Then they started to unload the raft. Kara hoped Robb was around. She was so excited she felt ready to pop!

"I have to go over to the cabin and check on something," Cy said. "Maybe you could look over all those valves while I'm gone. I'll be right back." He walked towards the cabin by the dock.

Kara knelt down and began to check the valves for each of the raft's air chambers. The air chambers inside a raft allowed it to be torn open by a rock without immediately sinking.

All at once Kara heard voices cheering. They were coming closer. She looked up. It was Robb, Cy, and all the guides. They were running towards her, cheering and waving. Suddenly they were all hugging her. "Congratulations, river guide!"

Then she felt herself being lifted up! Robb had her arms; Cy had her feet. They were heading towards the river. All the guides followed, yelling and cheering. Suddenly Kara knew what was happening. She was going to be dunked! Of course! Every new guide got dunked. It was an old rule on the river.

They had come to the edge of the dock. "OK now, Cy, are you ready?" Robb yelled. He and Cy started swinging Kara out over the water. "One, two, three!"

Kara felt herself flying through the air as everyone cheered. Then she landed in the icy cold water. But right now it felt wonderful. When she came back to the surface, she heard the guides clapping and saying her name. "Kara! Kara! Kara!" They were all lined up along the dock. Cy was holding up a big red beach towel for her. Kara forgot about the icy water. She just wanted to remember this moment forever.

The next morning Kara took her place at the oars of the raft. "Everybody ready?" She smiled at her three passengers, Mike, Ted, and Laura. They were a little older than she was.

"Are the rapids really bad? I've never done this before," Laura had told Kara earlier that morning.

"Don't worry at all. They're fun. You'll see. The first couple of times might seem a little bit rough. But after that you'll love it," Kara had said. She wondered if her passengers were worried about having a girl as their guide. This was something she'd never thought about before. What if people didn't want to do the river in her raft? Well, she'd have to show them she was just as good as anyone else.

"We'll go down the river in a group of three today," Kara told her passengers. "My brother Robb will be in the first raft. We'll follow him. Then the equipment raft will bring up the rear. We don't dare lose it—it's got our lunch!"

Kara looked over her raft one last time before she pushed away from the dock. She wanted to make sure she had all the important things. Extra life jackets, extra oars, the patch kit, first-aid kit, throw lines, bailing buckets. They were all there.

"Hey, kid, good luck today! Looks like a beautiful day to run the river." Cy was standing on the dock beside Kara's raft.

"We're gonna have a great run, aren't we, gang? See you later on, Cy." Kara smiled up at him as he pushed the raft away from the dock. She knew she owed him so much. It was hard to know how to thank somebody like Cy. He gave her his thumbs-up signal and stood watching as she eased the raft out into the current.

Kara rowed up beside Robb's raft. "We're all set. Lead the way!" She smiled at her brother.

"How about stopping for lunch at Big Oaks?" Robb called to her as he headed into the current.

"Sounds fine!" Kara loved the shady picnic spot under the huge old oak trees. She started to row slowly down the river. She left a distance of about thirty feet between her raft and Robb's.

Her raft was balanced well. It rode high and smooth on the gentle river. Laura and Mike sat in the bow, with Ted in the stern.

"How long have you been a guide?" Mike asked Kara.

"Not long. But I've been around this river most of my life. Three of my brothers have been guides." Kara somehow didn't want to tell Mike that this was her first real day as a guide.

"When will we get to the rapids?" Laura asked. She kept looking downstream.

"Pretty soon. I'll let you know when we get close. We'll be going into a pretty canyon ahead. Sometimes you can see eagle nests on the cliffs." Kara hoped the Chute wouldn't be too rough to-day. Last night's big rain had made the river higher. She'd been afraid Cy would cancel all runs for the day.

Suddenly Kara could hear the roar downriver. The Chute! She sucked in her breath and felt her muscles tense. This was it. She was in charge. Three people were depending on her to get them safely down the river.

"White water ahead! Coming into the canyon. Just sit tight and hold onto the safety lines." Kara put the raft in the center of the current and pointed her bow downstream. The river was high. The strong waves pulled the raft towards the canyon walls. Kara pushed hard on her oars. She kept thinking about what Cy had said that morning. "A big rain brings lots of changes to the river. Remember that. Keep your eyes open. There will be new holes, bigger waves, fallen trees. Don't count on anything being the same as it was yesterday."

"Kara kept her eye on Robb's raft as it raced down the Chute ahead of her. Sometimes she lost sight of him in the white spray that fell across the canyon.

Laura had bent down low in the bow. Mike had his arm around her as he held onto the safety line and stared down the Chute.

This is one of the worst runs. If they can get through this OK, the rest will seem easy. Except for the Graveyard, Kara thought. The high water would now be covering the tops of those boulders. That run could be deadly.

Suddenly they were out of the Chute. Now the raft rode easily in the waves. Laura sat up in the bow. "I'm soaked! Wow, that water's cold!"

"The sun will dry you off fast. This part of the trip is smooth. You can relax. Well, what do you think of the Chute?" Kara asked her passengers.

"Wow! I thought sure we were going to smash up on those canyon walls. You're great the way you handle this raft, Kara. I don't know how you do it." Ted shook his head and smiled at her.

Kara felt ten feet tall. "Thanks. Well, we're coming to a bend here. I've got to get to work." Kara began to ease the raft towards the inside shore. Her eyes searched the river ahead for fallen trees. They often got stuck in river bends. Getting snaggled in a fallen tree usually meant the end of a raft. The sharp branches could put a hole in every air chamber in seconds.

Kara guided the raft smoothly around the sharp bend. It felt good to have it behind her. Now she could think about the Graveyard. She could see Robb's raft heading towards the boulders. Then she lost sight of him. She waved to Al on the equipment raft as he came around the bend. Sure hope he's packed a good lunch today, Kara thought. I'm already starving.

Kara kept her raft to the center of the river as the Graveyard drew closer. She had to have total control when the current took hold of the raft in the white water ahead. I'm glad Laura doesn't know the name of this run, she thought. Laura had bent down in the bow again.

"Talk about boulders!" Ted shouted. "Holy smokes! There must be hundreds of them!"

Now Kara could see a huge green rock coming up dead ahead! Mike had seen it, too. "Look out! We're going to hit it," he yelled to Kara.

"No way," Kara yelled back above the roar of the rapids. She pushed hard on her oars and swung the raft neatly away from the rock and on down the river. She steered the raft from side to side, slipping around the boulders.

Was she getting too close to Robb's raft? Kara glanced farther down the river. Robb didn't seem to be in sight. Then—what was that? Kara felt her stomach go tight. Her throat felt as though it were about to close. Her heart began to pound. There, just ahead, was a raft slammed up against a boulder. She was sure it was Robb's. There was no one else on the river except for Al behind her. She had to get down there—fast! Somehow she steered her raft around the boulders. She rowed desperately toward her brother's raft. Her eyes searched the water for people. She saw no one. No one at all! Where was Robb? Then she saw him. He was pinned between the raft and the boulder!

Where was Robb? Then she saw him. He was pinned between the raft and the boulder!

CHAPTER 8

Pinned!

Was he alive? Had he passed out? Now Kara could see bodies bobbing down the river in their life jackets. Robb's passengers were in the icy cold water. Panic filled her. What should she do first—try to free Robb or go after the passengers? She knew they wouldn't live long in this icy water. Then she remembered the boat behind her. It could go after the other people. She could go after Robb. She waved her arms and yelled to Al to go on down the river.

"I'll get help!" he called to her as he raced past. "Don't worry. We'll get right back up here!" Then Al was gone.

She knew she had to pull into shore. But where? Suddenly she saw a small calm area behind some rocks next to the shore. She rowed towards it.

"Give me that rope!" Ted yelled to Kara. "I'll

tie the raft to that rock over there."

Kara threw Ted the rope and jumped out of the raft onto the shore. "Stay here, please, all of you. Don't leave the raft." Then she ran along the rocky shore towards Robb. How could it happen? Robb's the best guide on the river. But Cy's warning kept coming back. "A big rain brings lots of changes to the river. Never count on its being the same the next day."

Kara waded out to Robb. He was on his back with just his shoulders above water. His eyes were closed, and blood was running slowly down his face. There was a long ugly cut on his forehead. Kara pulled herself up onto the boulder. Its sides were steep and wet. She reached down to touch her brother. His skin was cold. But she could see a small vein moving on the side of his head. His heart was beating! He was still alive. Somehow she had to move the huge raft off his body.

Then she heard voices yelling from shore. Ted and Mike were running towards her. Kara had forgotten all about them. Now Ted was wading out towards the boulder. He was carrying a long rope. The rope! Maybe they could use it to pull the raft off Robb!

Mike waited on the shore since there was room

for only two people on the rock. Laura stayed at the raft.

"Is he alive?" Ted yelled as he pulled himself up beside Kara.

"Yes. Blacked out. The raft is crushing him. Got to get it off him. Let's try the rope. I'll tie it onto the raft. Then Mike can try pulling it from shore." Kara took the end of the rope and started inching her way down the steep rock. The first thing she touched was a safety line, and she tied the rope to this. Then Ted helped pull her back to the top of the rock. He carried the free end of the rope over to Mike. Then they both pulled hard on the rope. It was no use. The water pressure against the raft was too strong. Ted hurried back up onto the boulder.

Kara was desperate. They had to find some way to move that raft. She knew Robb would not live much longer if they didn't. She was sure he was suffering from hypothermia after being in the icy water for such a long time.

Suddenly Kara had an idea—let the air out of the raft's air chambers! Then maybe it could be moved. It was worth a try. There weren't many choices left. She told Ted what she planned to do.

"It's risky. Those valves look hard to reach.

But it just might work. Sure worth a try." Ted stared down at the raft. Then he added quietly, "Do you want me to do it?"

Kara heard fear in his voice. Perhaps he wasn't a strong swimmer. She saw him staring at the angry swift current racing by the boulder.

"No. I better do it, Ted. I know where the valves are. You just hold my legs while I reach down and try to unscrew the valves." Kara slowly began moving down the side of the boulder. Now she could see why the raft had been wrecked. Just below the surface of the water was a huge fallen tree. It must have blown down in the storm. Its sharp branches must have popped some air chambers in Robb's raft.

Kara's fingers found a valve at the top of the raft. But it was too tight to unscrew. She tried another valve. Same problem. Then she reached down into the icy water and tried one last valve. It wouldn't move. Kara was desperate. There was only one thing left to do. She reached for the knife she carried on her belt. Then she shoved it into a corner of the raft. Air raced out of the chamber. She plunged the knife in again. More air escaped. She kept slashing the raft until there was only one place left with air in it—the far right corner. She tried to pull Robb out. Surely the raft would let him go now. But he was still trapped.

Kara stared down at the corner of the raft that still had air in it. She couldn't reach it with her knife. Suddenly she had an idea. If she jumped down onto this part, maybe it would bounce the rest of the raft right off Robb! It was worth trying. First she had to get back up on top of the boulder. Ted helped pull her back up.

"Still can't move it. I'm going to try something else," Kara told Ted. "I'm going to jump down into the corner of the raft." She pointed down towards the water. "I think it'll lift this part of the raft right off Robb. Then you've got to grab him before he slides down into the water. OK?"

"What if you miss? You'll land right out in the current. You'll be swept downstream. Let's try the rope again first," Ted said.

"No. That's too slow. I'm going to try this. I think it'll work. Here goes!" Kara jumped down towards the raft's far right corner. She hit it just right! The rest of the raft lifted off Robb! Ted reached down and grabbed him. The damaged raft shot out into the swift current with Kara inside it. She knew she had to get free quickly. She *had* to get back to Robb and get him warmed up. Every second counted. There was no time to lose.

The current had already swept Kara at least fifty feet down the river. The raft was filled with icy water. She kicked free of it and let the current sweep her over to the far shore. She found a good place for getting out of the river. Then she raced along the bank till she was upstream of where Robb was.

There she went into the water and started swimming a strong sidestroke across the river. Her arms began to ache as she fought the swift current that tried to pull her downstream. Her body began to feel numb. She knew she had to keep going. The waves smacked into her face. Her mouth kept filling with water. Still she kept swimming, looking towards the shore where Robb was. At last she pulled herself out of the river and stumbled up onto the rocky shore. She could barely stand. She coughed up mouthfuls of cold river water. Her body was shaking, and she kept stumbling as she ran. Her legs didn't feel as though they belonged to her. The long swim in the icy water had taken its toll. Kara didn't know she was in the first stage of hypothermia herself. She just kept running towards Robb.

Ted, Mike, and Laura had laid Robb down on a sandy spot near the big boulder. They had covered him with jackets they found in the raft.

Kara threw herself down on the ground beside Robb. She lay there for a moment without moving.

"He's alive, Kara! He's still alive!" Ted knelt down beside her. "And you're half-dead. You swam that river. I can't believe you did it."

"He's alive, Kara! He's still alive!"

Kara slowly began to stop shaking. She was able to think more clearly. "Please. Build a fire. Quick," she said. Her mind was growing clearer by the second. She reached for Robb's wrist to feel his pulse. It was slow, very slow. She quickly began stripping off Robb's cold wet clothes. "Mike! Can you get me the blanket from the raft? Quick! It's in the big first-aid kit."

Kara lay down beside her brother and held his shaking body close to hers. His coldness made her start shaking again. Then Mike came back with the blanket and wrapped them both up tight inside it. Please let it work, Kara thought. How long would it be before someone would get down here and rescue them? Kara knew they were far from any road. Help would have to come down the river by raft.

Suddenly there was the sound of crackling wood. A fire! "Ted!" Kara called. "We've got to get something hot into Robb. Look in the first-aid kit. There's soup and cocoa."

"I'll go get it." Laura ran off towards the raft.

"Is he warming up?" Ted asked as he bent down towards Kara and Robb.

"I don't know. Hard to tell." Kara looked at her brother's face. The awful blue color was still there. She pulled Robb's body more tightly against her own.

CHAPTER 9

Six Weeks Later

It was six weeks later when Kara moved her raft slowly up to the river shore. This was the take-out place for all the rafts at the end of the day. She had dropped off her passengers at the dock. Suddenly she heard voices yelling in the parking lot. A car radio was turned up high. Then there was the sound of cheering. Robb came running down to the shore.

"Kara! Kara! We just heard! They're not going to build the dam after all! We've still got our river. And it's because of you!"

Kara stared at Robb. "Fantastic! What do you mean it's because of me?"

"You got that President's Award for Courage when you saved my life on the river. The whole country saw you on TV. You told about how the river would be lost if the dam was built. People started writing letters to the government. They wanted the river saved for rafting."

Cy came up behind Kara and gave her a bear hug. "You did it, kid! You got folks to notice us! Now we're going to be part of the National Wild and Scenic Rivers System. We'll never be dammed up!"

She felt dizzy with excitement. She couldn't believe it was all happening. In fact, the whole last six weeks had seemed like a dream. First the phone call from the President after he'd heard how she had rescued Robb. And then going to Washington to get the award. It all seemed unreal. It felt good now to be back on the river again. This was where she belonged. And now she knew there would be many summers of rafting ahead.

Suddenly all the guides started coming towards Kara and Robb.They were cheering and calling Kara's name. Robb lifted his sister to his shoulders while all the guides gathered around. Then he and Kara started off along the shore, leading a long parade of happy river people.